Song of
The Serial Kisser

A MYKE PHOENIX ADVENTURE

By Warren Bluhm

warrenbluhm.com

SONG OF THE SERIAL KISSER
A MYKE PHOENIX ADVENTURE

Cover image © Ponomarencko | Dreamstime.com

ISBN 978-1-7373499-8-3

Find the entire Myke Phoenix saga in *Myke Phoenix: The Complete Novelettes*, available wherever fine books are sold.

Prologue

THE great red-and-gold bird sailed high over the land, ever vigilant, ever wary. It's easy to grow lax over the course of a 500-year life span, but relaxation was not an option, not when a force of pure evil was afoot.

And knowing that force had not been vanquished, despite 18 years of intermittent struggle, was cause enough to stay vigilant. Someday a drooping of the head, a wandering of the mind, a distraction for a moment, would give the force an opening in the shield, and the resulting blow could be fatal for an entire planet.

The great bird's mission was to prevent that from opening. It could not permit itself a moment's diversion from the task at hand.

Its allies, after all, were mere flesh and blood.

And ceramic.

And so the great bird soared, and watched, and sang.

SONG OF THE SERIAL KISSER

Act 1
A stolen kiss, a weary hero

THE Astor City Mall bustled with weekend shoppers. There was a craft sale in the aisles – homemade jewelry and clocks made from old LPs and birdhouses and artfully decorated mailboxes, you know the stuff – and that made the shoppers crowd together even more.

Randi Vermiere had been shopping all afternoon, and she was happier than she had been for a while. This was going to be her boyfriend's best birthday ever, no doubt about it. She had only three small- to medium-sized bags to show for the effort, but what was inside those bags was exactly what he had asked for.

Everyone seemed to be in a good mood even though it wasn't anywhere close to Christmas. Maybe it was the fact that winter would soon be over. She even heard someone whistling the pretty opening notes of "Spring" from Vivaldi's "The Four Seasons."

Time to buy something for herself. She saw a man wearing sunglasses set up between the bookstore and yet another women's fashion shop. Roses! She deserved a rose.

"I'll take one of those," Randi chirped to the vendor, pointing at a container full of fragrant red roses.

"Which one are you looking at?" the man in the sunglasses asked, and she realized he was blind.

"I'm sorry," she said. "I'd like a red rose."

"All right, here you are," the vendor said, reaching for the correct vase and plucking a nice one out for her. "Don't they smell lovely?"

"Yes, they do," she laughed, exchanging cash for the flower. "That's why I had to have one. This is a five-dollar bill."

"Thank you," he said, and counted out the change. "The aroma matches your lovely voice."

"You're too nice," Randi replied and walked away, the rose just in front of her lips, enjoying the sweet springtime odor.

She turned up a back corridor to the parking lot when she felt him come up behind her and whisper, "You look so good in purple," then start nibbling on her neck.

Randi blushed and smiled and closed her eyes. Where had he come from? She didn't expect him to be at the mall today. The smell of the rose combined with the sensation on her neck was divine.

He turned her around and planted a gentle, warm kiss full on the lips that gave her a familiar longing feeling in the general vicinity of her belly. Eyes still closed, she gave a little moan of appreciation. Oh my, she loved the way he made her feel.

That's funny, he shaved his mustache, Randi realized, opening her eyes just a slit – and then as wide as could be.

The man kissing her so lovingly was not – in any way, shape or form – the man she expected to be kissing.

"What the – WHO ARE YOU?" she screamed. And she kept screaming as he laughed and fled down the corridor and into the parking lot.

Detective Captain Fredricks tried to call up the notes-taking app on his smartphone, swore under his breath, tucked the device into his coat pocket and retrieved a paper pad and pen.

"This works better for me anyway," he said apologetically. "So you thought it was your boyfriend."

"Well, who else is going to come up behind me like that and start kissing my neck?" Randi Vermiere asked innocently.

"Oh, gee, I don't know – a rapist? What were you thinking, girl?"

"It wasn't like that! He was very gentle and sweet, like Tom – my boyfriend's name is Tom. I was sure it was him," she said. "Except that it wasn't."

"Right. Did you get a good look at him?"

"Well, yes. Well, not so much. I was so surprised. He didn't have a mustache like Tom. I saw that it wasn't Tom's mouth, and screamed, and he ran. The rest of his face, I don't know."

"Could you pick the guy out of a lineup if you had to?"

"Maybe," she said not so confidently. "His mouth, at least."

"Right. And you'd just bought a rose from the blind guy at the kiosk. Did you notice anyone hanging around, maybe watching you?"

"No, I was looking at the rose."

"I mean before, while you were shopping, did you see the same guy looking at you at different places?"

"Not really – I tune that out. Guys are always looking, you know what I mean?"

She was a good-looking girl. "Yeah, I know what you mean. OK, here's my card, if you think of anything –anything that might help us find the guy – give me a call. Especially if you think of something besides his mouth not looking like Tom's."

"He had a brown coat on."

"Cloth or leather?"

"Fabric."

"That's good. Blue jeans or business pants?"

"Pants. Brown pants. Kind of casual pants, not real business-like. And he had a nice laugh, it wasn't like a mean laugh. He was a good kisser. I hate to say that, but he kissed as good as Tom does. It was very nice, except for I didn't want to kiss him."

This was not going to be easy. A clean-shaven guy with brown casual pants and a brown coat. Could be anybody. The blind vendor remembers selling the rose to her. He obviously didn't see anybody nearby. Nobody saw the kiss, nobody saw the guy running away, they just heard the scream.

In this state kissing a lady who doesn't want to get kissed is not a felony. They call it fourth-degree sexual assault, which sounds serious but it's a misdemeanor with a $50 fine and maybe 15 days in jail max. A stolen kiss not generally an offense that brings out a captain of the detective squad to investigate.

The reason Fredricks was on the case was that it was the 27th stolen kiss in the last two weeks. The description in each incident was as vague as this one, but they all sounded like the same guy – sudden and unwelcome, but gentle and even nice.

"A serial kisser," Fredricks muttered. "What a freakin' waste of time this is."

The whole thing was perplexing. The guy had managed to find 27 public places where he could walk up to an unsuspecting woman and plant a big, wet one on them, or as big and as wet a kiss as they would allow. Even when he was caught on surveillance camera, he managed to keep the system from getting a good look at his face. The ladies were shaken up, some to the point of becoming anxious when their boyfriends or husbands approached them romantically, but there wasn't an overwhelming demand to track the guy down and press charges.

Fredricks was the only detective who thought it would be worthwhile to pursue the thing.

"What if he takes it farther than stealing a kiss?" he asked. "At some point maybe kissing her isn't going to be enough of a thrill."

"Well, that's why it would be nice to catch him, to make sure he doesn't," District Attorney Kenneth Ronnegan Jr. had said. "But in the meantime we have bigger fish to fry. Don't waste the resources."

The resources. The personnel. The damn budget. Once upon a time the cops just worried about catching the bad guys, protecting and serving. Now it was all about prioritization. Fredricks hadn't plucked a kitten out of a tree for a little kid for about 30 years, not while he was on the clock at least. What was the world coming to?

Maybe tracking down a serial kisser wasn't going to be his top priority. But he'd get the guy before he did any real harm. Or maybe an angry boyfriend would get to him first.

"Astor County Sheriff's Dispatch, Blanche speaking."

"Hey, it's Paul Phillips. How are ya, Blanche?"

"Nothing going on, Paul."

"What? No hot dates or anything?"

"Very funny. No, I ain't been seeing anyone lately."

"Don't worry, someone will come along. Say, anything worth writing for the news overnight?"

"I told you, nothing going on."

"You said that when I asked 'how are ya.' Now I'm asking if anything happened overnight."

"You're what, like a comedian? Have a nice day."

Someday he would get Blanche the dispatcher to lighten up. But today was not going to be that day.

Paul Phillips was the editor, reporter, typist, heck, he was the whole staff of the Astor City Beacon news blog. Once a hotshot radio news reporter, he was laid off when WACR decided that having a local news team was too expensive. He spent a few years with the Astor City Tribune until it decided that modern times required getting by with one-third of the news staff it had back in the day. Unwilling to give up his lifetime urge to tell people what was going on in their town, he eked out a living applying his journalistic skills online.

"It's hard to write up a news update when there's no news going on," he grumbled, apparently to himself.

"Don't look so disappointed, Paul. It's good news – the forces of evil in the world took the night off."

The new voice appeared to be coming from an ugly green vase on a bookshelf. The voice had a somewhat feminine but definitely male tone to it, and the vase was pale green with the painted figure of a red bird and crystal, red and blue glass jewels embedded around the top and bottom.

Perhaps the most amazing thing about this scene is that Paul Phillips did not seem to be especially surprised to hear a disembodied voice coming from the general vicinity of a butt-ugly green vase on his bookshelf.

Did I mention that in addition to being a hotshot reporter, for the last 18 years Paul Phillips had led a double life as Myke Phoenix, superhero and protector of Astor City? The vase was the Soulkeeper of Kiribati, and when bad guys threatened, Paul exchanged his everyday reporter's pudgy body for the invulnerable frame of a mighty warrior named Mychus.

"Yes, it's great that the forces of evil took the night off, but I got nothin' and people will start logging in for news in a little while," he told the vase.

"Are you talking to the furniture again?" came a third voice, this one definitely feminine. It belonged to a good-looking woman of a certain age with bright blue eyes, auburn hair with a hint of gray here and there – or were they highlights? – who walked into the room stretching and wearing a robe.

"The babe awakes. Hiya, doll." This was the odd voice in the vase, not Paul Phillips.

"Hello, ugly," she replied, this to the ugly vase, not Paul Phillips. At the beginning of their relationship, Paul was the only one who could hear the vase's voice. Early on the vase decided it was all right for the wife to listen in.

Dana Dunsmore Phillips had been Paul's partner for a little more than two decades and his wife for the last 15 of those years. Truth be told, she had evolved into the breadwinner of this little family as the owner of one of the biggest public relations/marketing companies in Astor City. Her company was a major sponsor of the Astor City Beacon, and she helped secure other sponsors when she wasn't putting out fires, managing people and otherwise running D.S. Dunsmore Advertising Agency.

"So did anybody get shot last night?" Dana asked Paul the way an average person might ask, "Who won the ballgame?"

"No," Paul replied ruefully. "It's one slow news day already."

"You got that United Way interview from the other day, you could write that up quick," she said. "Did you remember to make coffee today?"

"Yeah, have some," he said. "I forgot about that interview, thanks – I can make something out of that pretty quick."

"Whatever happened to the powerful forces of evil in the universe?" she asked the vase cheerfully. "This town has been pret-ty darn quiet lately."

"What, are you complaining? That used to be a good thing, evil taking the week off," the vase said. "Careful what you wish for."

"Evil can take the week off anytime," Dana said. "We haven't had a supervillain invade town for – at least a couple of years, isn't it?"

"I'd guess the Grasshopper Bandit was the last time we had a guy that nobody except Myke could handle, and that was two summer ago," Paul agreed. "It's kind of depressing."

"You're depressed because you chased off the Forces of Evil? I don't believe this," the vase said, and if it had lungs it would have exhaled in exasperation. "Don't worry, dummy, the Forces of Evil don't stay chased."

"Is something brewing?" Paul said almost expectantly.

"Just the coffee," the green thing said. "What are you depressed about?"

"I don't know," he said. "Deinonychus is out of the picture. Prince Cormorant was deposed, and he's in exile in Switzerland with none of the power and resources he used to have. It's the same with all of the really bad guys we've fought over the years. Lately it's just been everyday crooks and the occasional mobster. And even then, there's nobody like Alan Pinkstaff who almost ran the town with his crime syndicate. It just seems like we don't need Myke Phoenix anymore."

"You say that like it's a bad thing," Dana said, running her hands across his shoulders. "That's a victory, you big idiot. You're winning."

"I guess. Maybe that is a good thing, after 18 years even being a superhero gets a little old," Paul said, staring vacantly at his computer screen, and then starting. "I'd better write up that interview."

"If it's any consolation, the Forces of Evil never go away completely. They'll be back," the vase said. "And it'll happen just when you don't want them to."

"Can they come back soon? I need a story," Paul said, a slight twinkle returning to his eye.

"Don't push your luck." The vase went silent, Dana read the news on her smartphone, and the clickadee-clack of Paul's keyboard telling the United Way story was the only sound in the room for the next half-hour.

Act 2
The usual suspects

SONNY Boneau fidgeted at the table in the interview room. He heard the murmur of cops talking on the other side of the door, and he thought he heard the clunk of a coffee cup being set down on a counter behind the big glass that everybody knew was a one-way mirror so other cops could watch the proceeding. Sonny figured he'd been sitting by himself for at least 15 minutes.

"Come *on*," he hollered. "Let's get this over with. I ain't got all day."

He kind of jumped when his holler was met by the abrupt opening of the door. Detective Captain Fredricks walked in.

"Fredricks!" Sonny said with some surprise. "What'd I do? I thought you was riding a desk these days."

"Not so much," Fredricks replied. "How are you, Sonny? Do any break-ins lately?"

"No! I did my time and I'm clean now," the burglar replied. Both men knew it wasn't true, but Sonny hadn't been caught lately. "What are you trying to pin on me?"

"Well, I got a weird one I'm working on, and you strike me as weird," the detective captain deadpanned. "Do you know we have a serial kisser in town?"

Sonny Boneau sputtered. "A serial killer? I ain't no murderer. No way."

Fredricks smirked.

"Kisssser," he said, drawing out the "s" sound in the middle of the word. "We have a serial kisssser in town. Walks up to ladies and plants one on them."

"He just kisses them?" It was Sonny's time to smirk. "How 'bout that. Good for him!"

"No, not good. It's illegal to kiss a stranger without their permission."

"I still say good for him. Some girls need to be kissed."

"Not. Like. This," Fredricks said. "You like the idea so much, maybe it's you I'm lookin' for."

"What?" Flabbergasted. "No, that's not my style."

"Whose style is it?" Fredricks said. "Because you know, the way he cases places, picks where to do his thing without being picked up on security cameras, the

M.O. sure reminds me of a talented burglar or robber. Yep, it does."

"What are you talking about?"

Fredricks was talking about having a conversation with anyone and everyone he'd ever busted for breaking and entering, shoplifting, or otherwise taking advantage of an innocent victim. After the kisser's victim list hit 20, Fredricks had spent the week shaking down the petty criminals of Astor City and asking them about the Serial Kisser.

And after a while, they began to get irritated. More about that later, because first I need to describe the 28th incident.

Rollie's Bar was one of those bars that, six weeks later, you and your friends are saying "What was the name of that bar we went to that night?" and darned if any of you can remember it. Pick a bar, any bar you've been in. Yeah, it was that kind of bar.

On the end of the bar sat a woman. Pick a woman you've seen at a bar and thought, hey, she's not bad. Not too pretty, but definitely not unpleasant to look at. Yeah, that was her.

Rhoda Tennyson was sitting at the end of the bar at Rollie's, pretty much minding her own business. She wanted to be alone. If someone came up and offered to buy her a drink, she might have said yes, but she was hoping nobody would offer. She wasn't horribly depressed or anything; sometimes you just want to be left alone and have a drink by yourself. Rollie's was one of those places where maybe a girl could do that. And sure enough, it wasn't a busy night, and she was most of the way through her metropolitan and feeling like it was a good night to be alone. A guy whistling some classical thing, Vivaldi maybe, walked past behind her and into the men's room.

"'Nother one?" asked the bartender.

"No, I'm good," Rhoda replied. He nodded and walked to the other end, where there were glasses to clean and dry.

The men's room door opened and closed. Rhoda picked up her glass and gazed blankly at the mirror, watching a guy walk most of the way past her, but then he leaned around and give her a kiss.

"Hey!" she said, wiping her mouth. "What was that all about?"

The man was already past the bartender, who looked around and saw the back of the guy's head, then turned back to Rhoda.

"What happened? You all right?"

"He kissed me! Just all of a sudden kissed me."

"What'd you say to him?"

"Nothing! He just up and kissed me."

"Doesn't sound so bad."

"It wasn't so bad, that's not the point!"

"I suppose not."

"Where did he go?" Rhoda asked, looking past the bartender. He followed her line of sight.

"Gone. I think he walked right out."

"Well, I'm calling 9-1-1."

"What, this is an emergency?"

"Rueben, the guy kissed me. Who knows what he's thinking of doing next?"

The 9-1-1 dispatcher transferred the call to Detective Captain Fredricks, who ended his conversation with Sonny Boneau and drove down to Rollie's Bar.

Rhoda Tennyson was not the most cooperative victim ever. She had just wanted to finish her metropolitan and go home to her cats. The more she talked about it, the less she wanted to talk about it.

"How about you?" Fredricks asked Rueben the bartender. "You get a look at the guy?"

"He was kind of in a hurry, walking past me already when the lady yelled," Reuben said. "All I saw was the back of his head."

You know that face people make when they want to swear but they decide to do it silently? Kind of a sudden downward jerk of the head and a grunt. That's what Fredricks did now.

That was fun. She looked so surprised. Seemed like a nice lady, all by herself. A woman needs to feel like she's not all by herself, like somebody noticed she's cute and kissable.

Why do I do that? They're always a little mad when I do that. I probably shouldn't do that.

But that was fun.

The man walked along Seventh Avenue, whistling the "Spring" theme from "The Four Seasons."

Paul and Dana Phillips didn't get out together much. He was always reporting the news or fighting evil, and she was waist-deep in running her business. They had to schedule a date to spend time together. The good news is they made a point to go on a date at least once a week, but it often involved popcorn and wine in front of the television set at home, watching an old movie.

Getting to Radicchio's was a special treat for both of them. The Italian restaurant was famous for its exotic salads and fabulous pasta creations, and the music was subdued enough that they could carry on an intelligent conversation.

They were in the middle of such a conversation when Paul spotted a familiar face over her shoulder. The face was passing by behind Dana, so rather than excuse himself and walk over, he simply called out.

"Bo! Bo Ranfort!"

The tall, well-dressed man looked in his direction, and his expression lit up.

"Paul! Dana! How the heck are you guys?"

Ranfort was the former owner/manager of WACR Radio, the Voice of the Community, which until just a few years ago had lived up to its slogan by providing 24 hours of locally produced programs including locally reported, locally announced news. After he sold the station and retired, well, remember I mentioned that Paul left WACR and became a newspaper reporter? That was after Bo Ranfort sold the station and retired.

After the usual pleasantries – Bo was with his wife, Candi – they got to talking about the old place.

"It's really gone to hell, hasn't it?" Ranfort admitted sheepishly. "I suppose I shouldn't have retired, but you just have to step away at some point."

"Not your fault, Bo, it's the business," Paul said. "They never found another talk show rabble rouser like Hi Dawson, so they hitched their star to a satellite dish like everyone else."

"I told that SOB to lay off the cigarettes, but he didn't listen to anybody," Bo said.

"Not his style," Paul agreed.

Bo and Candi had very nice things to say about the Astor City Beacon blog, and they agreed it was nice that the snow was melting and the days would be really warming up sometime soon, and then the Phillips' order arrived and the Ranforts went off to their own table.

"It's good to see Bo," Paul said wistfully. "He really was a throwback, and so was his radio station."

"You'd think he could have let people in the community know the station was for sale instead of selling out to that big chain," Dana said with a frown. "The advertising reps lost all of their ability to make a deal – if I've heard 'That's not the company's policy anymore' once, I've heard it 100 times."

"Isn't that the way of the world nowadays," Paul said, more of a comment than a question. "They make it easy to say, 'Sorry, it's out of my control, there's nothing I can do about it.'"

The food was great as always, and they each were with their favorite person, so the rest of the evening went comfortably. As Paul figured out the tip, Dana excused herself to go to the ladies' room.

She was relaxed and happy. Business was doing all right, Paul's venture and adventures were progressing, and the calendar's promise of coming spring takes the edge off the end of winter. Dana smiled; as she passed the men's room door she heard someone whistling Vivaldi.

The reader should not be surprised at this point to learn that when she was finished in the ladies room and stepped back into the corridor, Dana became the 29th woman in Astor City to be accosted by an overly affectionate stranger.

"Did he hurt you?" Paul asked earnestly.

"I'm fine, it wasn't a rough kiss, just – sudden," Dana said, and lowered her voice so only Paul could hear: "If I was in any danger, you would have turned into Myke automatically."

That much was true – Mychus the Warrior was known to switch bodies with Paul all of a sudden, seconds before an attack of some kind.

"What if he's some terrorist spreading germs?" Paul said. "I don't like this at all."

Dana shot him a look of extreme skepticism. "Terrorist? Really?"

Detective Captain Fredricks arrived at the restaurant just then. He and Paul eyed each other with surprise.

"How'd you find out about this?" the detective asked.

"Captain Fredricks, meet my wife, Dana. She's your complainant. Why did the police send a detective – a detective captain! – on this case?" the reporter asked.

"Pleased to meet you. I was in the neighborhood," Fredricks said. "That, and the fact that this guy has done this to a couple dozen other women in the last two-three weeks."

"What!" Paul said. "There's like a, serial kisser on the loose?"

"Don't be so freakin' dramatic," Fredricks said, a little irked that the reporter had come up with the same phrase as he. "It's a misdemeanor. Kind of weird that he's doing it so often, but nobody's –"

"That's not the point, Captain. Don't you think people might want to know that this is going on? Why didn't you tell us in the media about this?"

Because you'd blow it out of proportion and scare women more than they deserve to be scared, Fredricks thought.

"I don't feel like causing a panic over this," Fredricks said out loud. "You mind if I interview the victim here, old buddy? Did you get a good look at the guy, Mrs. Phillips?"

"Dana. Not really. I was just coming out of the ladies room, and he sort of swooped by, took me by the shoulders and gave me a big kiss."

"Did you see his eyes, his nose, what he was wearing?"

"Brown eyes, actually kind of friendly look to his face. His nose was sort of hooked, and he had a round chin. Clean shaven. Brown overcoat, casual brown pants."

Fredricks' eyes widened a bit. That was the most detailed description any of the 29 women had given so far. She was very observant. Maybe being a reporter's wife ...

"I thought you said you didn't get a good look at him."

"I notice details."

"Would you object to sitting down with a sketch artist?"

"I suppose not."

"I thought this wasn't a big deal," Paul Phillips said sarcastically.

"Compared to 29 murders, it isn't a big deal," Fredricks said. "But this is upsetting to the people involved."

"Darn right it is," Paul grumbled. "I can't believe you've been covering this up."

"Shush, Paul," Dana said. "He had his reasons. And now you know."

SONG OF THE SERIAL KISSER

And the next morning, the readers of the Astor City Beacon news blog knew, too.

Act 3
The pact

A half-dozen shady-looking guys sat around a half-dozen bottles of beer and a basket of popcorn at one of those bars like Rollie's Bar. Only it wasn't Rollie's, it was – actually, no one remembers which bar exactly it was. The important thing was, Sonny Boneau and five other shady-looking guys were having a beer.

"This Serial Kisser SOB ain't good for our business," Sonny was saying.

"You got that right," one of the other guys, Ted Rademacher, said bitterly. "Jeez, Fredricks hauled me in the other day just because I did some time for robbery. Said this guy has the same M.O. I never kissed anybody I ripped off!"

"Ya dummy, it's the way he sneaks up on them like we sneak up on a mark," Jimmy Dehn said. "It's like he thinks one of us graduated from grabbing purses to kissin' the broads?"

"It's bad for business," Sonny repeated. "First off, the cops are walking the streets more. Second off, people are getting more cautious. It's like they don't mind if we steal their wallets, but oh hey, don't kiss me – that's a step too far, don't ya know."

As Fredricks had feared, the media was running with the "Serial Kisser" mania. It wasn't so much Phillips' blog, it was the TV stations. They were playing it cute, but they were also getting people riled up. It didn't help that he had now surprised more than 40 women with a sudden public display of unwanted affection.

"You know what we need to do?" Sonny Boneau said. "We gotta stop him ourselves."

"What?!" said Scarface Mahoney, who was a skinny 19-year-old pickpocket who got scratched by an overly affectionate yellow lab when he was a kid. "We're not the cops."

"Once the Serial Kisser is put out of business, people will calm down and they'll go back to carrying their purses loose and forgetting to lock their doors," Sonny said.

"You know, that actually makes sense," Jimmy said. "You think we should get the word out to watch for the guy?"

"Yeah, I do," Sonny said.

"Maybe we could recruit some of the boyfriends or husbands," Ted said. "They're pretty ticked off about it."

Sonny Boneau looked at Ted Rademacher with sincere admiration. "Teddy, that's the best idea you've had in 10 years. Yeah, of course those guys are gonna be motivated."

"But what are we going to do with the guy if we catch him?" Scarface asked.

The question hung in the air for a few seconds.

"We'll figure that out when we get him," Sonny said.

Paul Phillips emerged from the clerk of courts office and was heading down to a courtroom to watch a gentleman who was going to be sentenced for his 11th conviction of operating a motor vehicle while intoxicated.

"Mr. Phillips?" came a low voice nearby. He turned and saw a short man with a few days' worth of beard and a baseball cap pulled almost over his eyes.

"Can I help you?"

"Maybe, if you got a minute. I hear your lady got kissed by that nutcase last week."

That got Paul's attention. "Do you know something about it?"

"Just what I see on TV." That always irritated Paul more than it should; the TV reporters usually saw it on the Beacon first and then ran with the story as their own. "But a bunch of guys are working to catch the moron on our own."

"What guys? What's wrong with letting the police do their jobs?"

"It ain't a top priority for them, and you know that," the unshaven man said. "Anyway, it's some of us guys and we're thinking the boyfriends might want to help us look. And you with your connections inside the cop shop …"

"Look, I wouldn't risk the trust I've built up with the police over the years by sharing stuff other than what's in the stories I write," Paul said.

"Yeah, yeah, I'm just asking if you hear anything or see anything that would help us catch him, tell us too."

Paul considered the suggestion. If he knew how to catch the serial kisser, he'd probably take care of the little creep himself in his Myke Phoenix uniform. But if there was some weird vigilante group forming, that might be an interesting story of its own.

"How would I find you?"

"Oh, I'm here a lot, I have a few cases pending, if you get my drift," the man said. "I'll watch out for you and we can talk here."

"Do you think your leaders would be willing to comment on the record for a story?" Paul asked, and he got a look as if he were a space alien. "I'll take that as a 'no.'"

Geoff Rogers was a little angrier than usual, but he refused to let it show. It didn't help business when he wasn't the sweet and cheerful blind man who sold flowers at the Astor City Mall.

It's not as if he didn't have a good reason for being angry. His friend Yancy took a look at Geoff's cashbox every couple of hours, and it was in disarray when he checked a few minutes ago. There were $5 bills mixed in with the twenties, and $10 bills with the ones. Obviously one or more customers had lied about what they were handing him, and at least one or more had lied when he inadvertently gave them more change than he should have.

Who would take advantage of a blind man? He wanted to fume and rant and rave, but he knew he had to project the cheerful front. Thank goodness Yancy was there to catch stuff like this.

"Calm down, relax, sell your flowers," Geoff said to himself. A shopper walked by whistling. "Be like that person, carefree, happy to serve."

"Can I buy one of these roses?" a soft feminine voice asked.

"You can buy as many as you like," Geoff smiled broadly. "Here, don't they smell lovely?"

"Oh, they surely do," she replied. A slight Southern accent. "But just the one will do."

"All right, that's two-fifty," he said.

"Here you are," the woman said, handing him a single bill.

"Is this a five?" Geoff asked.

"Oh, I'm sorry, it's a ten."

It *better* be a ten, he thought, handing her two quarters, two $1 bills and a $5 bill in change. He trusted his customers and folded each bill in a special way so he could tell them apart. But it all depended on them being honest.

"There you go," he said cheerfully. "The aroma goes perfectly with your lovely Tennessee voice."

"How did you know I'm from Tennessee?" she asked in delighted surprise.

"You sound like a southern belle," Geoff smiled.

Four minutes later, there was a commotion down the corridor not far from Geoff Rogers' kiosk. The southern belle had received an unexpected kiss in a side hallway.

"Just like a week or so ago," Geoff mused to himself, and then he made a connection.

Someone had been whistling just before the Tennessee woman walked up. Before that first incident, someone had walked past the flower stand whistling the same tune – some classical thing. You don't suppose – seems like a weird coincidence – but if it *was* a coincidence, he wouldn't want to get someone in trouble. But what are the odds? Two times he had heard someone whistling that tune, two stolen kisses a few minutes later.

He thought he'd mention it if the police came around asking about the southern belle. They didn't come around. But he did mention it to Yancy. It turns out that Yancy was a friend of Sonny Boneau.

"Sonny?" Yancy purred into his cellphone. "I think I might have a clue for you."

The blind vendor whistled the tune to Yancy, who recognized the melody.

"It's the 'spring' theme from 'The Four Seasons,'" he told Sonny. "You know, Vivaldi."

"Va-who?" Boneau asked.

"Oh come on, you know: Da-dum-dum-dum-dada-DOO, Dada-dum-dum-dum-dada-DOO, dada-dum-dada-dum-dum-dum," he sang.

"Huh. Yeah, I guess I've heard that riff before," Boneau said.

And the word went out.

The Astor City Mall was bustling with people that evening, and Geoff Rogers was doing good business. The roses always sold like gangbusters, but everything else was also moving. With spring just around the corner, people were snapping up the potted daffodils, too. He was so busy he almost didn't hear it.

Across the corridor. Someone whistling. Not just whistling, but whistling that little classical cadence, the one Yancy said was from Vivaldi.

"Are you still there, young man?" Geoff called out.

Scarface Mahoney had been hanging around near Geoff Rogers' flower kiosk for two or three hours and he was really, really bored. But he heard it, too, and his heart started pumping a little harder.

"Yeah. Was that him?" Scarface said, scanning the crowd.

"It sure sounded like the same guy," Geoff said, pointing. "Over that way."

"On it."

Scarface walked briskly in the direction of the whistling, and it wasn't too long before he matched the sound with the back of a head. Brown hair, not too light, not too dark. But the whistle made him.

A blond-haired woman turned down the back corridor toward the parking lot. A few steps behind her, the whistling man also turned down the back corridor.

"No way," Scarface Mahoney muttered, and picked up his pace.

She had a bag slung over a shoulder and was carrying shopping bags in both hands. The shoulder bag's straps looked easy to snap. If only Scarface was looking to grab a purse, it looked easy. But that wasn't the goal here. The man had stopped whistling and was only about five steps behind the blonde, but he glanced back and saw Scarface and slowed his pace.

The young thug slapped the man on the shoulder and saw that he was in his late twenties, beak nose, round chin.

"Hey buddy, are you wearing a watch? I wonder what time it is."

The guy, looking a little put out, pulled a cellphone from his coat pocket and lit the screen. "7:22." He patted his pants pocket as if to make sure his wallet was still there. Ahead, the door to the parking lot closed behind the blonde.

"Great. Thanks," Scarface said, spinning and heading back up the corridor. Just around the corner, he pulled out his own phone.

"Hey, Sonny, it's Scarface. I got him. Astor City Mall, right now he's in the east back corridor. Whoop! He's back in the mall," he said, turning his back on the whistling man.

"I'll make some calls. Keep an eye on him," Sonny said.

"Don't worry, I will," Scarface replied. "And I slapped the tag on him, too."

Damn kid, asking me what time it is. Why me? I was almost on her. It was going perfect. Probably a pickpocket; good thing I heard him and turned my wallet pocket away from him at the last second.

She was a pretty one, too. It would have been fun.

The challenge had increased in the week since that blog first revealed what he was doing. Funny that the police took so long to announce what he was doing. Being famous was part of the fun, he had to admit, but women were harder to find alone now, too.

That stuff about "we hope this doesn't escalate into something serious" was just rubbish, too. All he wanted was to kiss ladies. After all, women need to be kissed, and often, and by someone who knows how. It was fun, and most of them didn't seem to mind so much.

He whistled. The "spring" theme from "The Four Seasons." Spring was coming soon, and the ladies would start wearing their spring and summer clothes. It'd be easier to smell their scent then, and they'd be warmer to the touch.

It had been 20 minutes or so since that stupid kid broke up the opportunity. He walked past the flower kiosk. If he didn't know any better, he'd swear the blind guy was watching him go by. Whatever.

That little woman wearing the beret looks cute. Some people call that mousy hair, but I like it, especially with the beret as an accent. She turned down the back corridor. *Perfect.*

"Hey buddy, what's that on your back?"

Now what!?

"You talking to me?"

"Yeah, you've got some sort of sticker on your left shoulder."

He reached over his shoulder, and sure enough, there was a sticker there.

"What do you know. Thanks."

"No problem."

It was one of those name tag stickers that says "My name is." But it didn't have a name on it, just one letter.

"K."

He stared at the tag in dumb silence for a second. Where'd *this* come from? He looked around and saw the kid who had asked for the time about 50 feet away. He had two or three friends with him. Big, tough-looking friends.

He must have stuck the tag on when he slapped my shoulder. Why? What's this all about.

"K."

A TV commercial jingle incongruously spun through his head: "Every kiss begins with K."

He turned away from the kid and his thuggish buddies and saw three other thugs walking meaningfully in his direction.

"K." K for Kisser. Oh. My. God.

He ran. Two sets of brutes ran after him.

Act 4
The trial

"ASTOR County Dispatch, Blanche speaking."

"Hey Blanche, it's Paul Phillips."

"You just don't quit, do you?"

"I'm like clockwork, good lady. Every morning at 4:45, it's call the 911 dispatch center. And ask what's going on. You know that."

"Nothing going on, same as always."

"Nothing? Not even another kiss from the Serial Kisser?"

"Nope, he took the night off. The only thing we heard about the Kisser was a phony report that he'd been abducted."

"You're kidding."

"Yeah, somebody said there was a bunch of guys ganged up on someone and tossed him in a van, and another call said they were yelling about 'We caught the Kisser,' but when the squad got there, there was no sign of a van or the kids who called it in. Figure it was a prank.”

“Probably. Where was this?”

“Down the street from the mall. That’s the thing, the responding officers couldn’t find anyone who actually saw this happen. Like I said, it was just kids in the mall playing games. No news for you, even if I wanted to give you some, which I don’t.”

“Thanks, Blanche, you’re a peach.”

The guy with the baseball cap was walking the hall at the courthouse. Paul caught his eye.

“Hey. Anything new to report out there?” Paul asked.

“I was looking for you,” the cap said. “You want a piece of him?”

“A piece of who?”

“You know who.”

“I think I know who, but what are you talking about?”

“They caught him. The guys caught him, the guys I told you about. You didn’t hear this from me.”

“I protect my sources with the best of them.”

“Five o’clock this afternoon, the old Astor Brewery. You can have a piece of him, get him back for what he did to your girlfriend.”

"What, you're going to beat him up or something?"

"Whatever you want. Just saying. We're going to have a little trial, gotta have due process, you know. Then everyone can take a piece of him."

"You're not worried the police will find out about this?"

"Who's going to tell? You protect your sources, right?"

The hood was finally removed, and then the duct tape, rudely.

The face underneath had brown eyes, a beak-like nose, and a round chin.

"That's him," a female voice said, emphatically, over in the corner.

"Yes. It is him," another feminine voice said, assuredly.

"What *is* this?" the man said. But the look on his face betrayed that he knew what it was, or at least that he knew why the two women said what they said.

His hands were tied behind his back, and he had been placed in a chair. There was a light over him, but he had been in darkness for something like 18 hours, so he couldn't see right away. Once his eyes adjusted, he saw there were about 30 men across the room, and four, no, five women off to the side. The women all were nodding. And he recognized them all.

"That's him," Randi Vermiere said, although he didn't know that was her name. "I didn't think I'd recognize him, but that's definitely him."

"Why am I here?" he said.

Sonny Boneau sat at a table in front of the men. (He didn't know Sonny, but you and I do, so I'm telling you to make it easier on us.) He snorted at the question.

"You know why you're here," Sonny said, and he whistled the first few notes of the "Spring" theme from Vivaldi's "The Four Seasons."

The Serial Kisser gasped as if hearing his own whistle for the first time.

"What – what are you going to do?"

"Make you stop," Sonny said.

"HOW?"

"Well, that's up to you, isn't it? You've upset these women, and some of these men, their boyfriends and husbands. You've upset the rest of us by bringing the law down on the streets harder than usual. We're upset, mister. We're very upset. And it's time for you to stop."

"Please! I haven't hurt anyone," the Kisser whimpered. "It's just a little fetish. I can't help myself!"

"You haven't hurt anyone?" This was one of the men behind Sonny. "I can't touch my girl without her jumping like I'm some kind of wild animal or a rapist or something. You did that to her, creep."

The crowd started to move in. He stood, awkwardly, because his hands were bound behind his back.

"Please!" he said, more of a shriek than a whimper now. "I want to stop – but I can't. I can't resist the impulse. You have no idea what it's like. I just have to kiss someone!"

"Well, maybe if we rearranged your kisser," the closest man said. And he slugged him, reeling him back a step.

"And maybe if we made sure it doesn't escalate into something worse," the next-closest man said. And he kicked him in the groin.

"Yeah!" the group roared.

More than a handful of the men stepped from the crowd then, surrounding the man, who fell to his knees holding his hands to his head in a feeble attempt to protect himself.

"OK, boys, that's enough," a strong baritone voice barked.

The voice belonged to a very tall, blond-haired man with a chest shaped like a barrel, who stepped in front of the frantic kisser. He was wearing a white uniform with buttons down the side of the tunic. The image of a red-and-gold bird was emblazoned on his chest.

"Hokey smokes," someone in the back of the room said. "That's Myke Phoenix."

"I don't care if it's the governor," the groin-kicker said. "This guy's going to pay." And he wound up his leg for another wallop.

Myke intercepted the flailing leg and flipped the man head over heels. He landed with a belly flop and a burst of dust on the floor of the abandoned brewery.

"Go home, folks, I'll bring this guy to the police station," Myke told the surly crowd.

"He's just gonna get off with probation or something," someone shouted.

"We'll let the judge sort that out," the big warrior said, "but I imagine he'll order some mental health treatment while he's at it."

The group started to file slowly out of the building. The wail of police sirens approaching the building sped up the process. Paul Phillips protected his sources of information, but he wasn't going to stand by and let 30 angry men take care of the Serial Kisser.

As the room emptied, Myke grabbed Sonny Boneau, Scarface Mahoney and the other folks who had met around some beers and said, "Hang on just a second, fellas."

"What did we do?" Sonny demanded.

"Let's see, kidnapping, false imprisonment, battery ... for starters," Myke replied. "And boys? It's still not safe for burglars and robbers on the streets of this town."

He turned to the Serial Kisser, who was looking at him with a grateful expression, and began to untie his bindings.

"I could just kiss you," the man said.

"Don't push your luck."

SONG OF THE SERIAL KISSER

Epilogue

DANA pulled back after one of the most luscious kisses in the history of kisses, definitely somewhere in the Hot 100.

"What was that for?" Paul asked, holding her close so that their lips were in close proximity in case she wanted to dive in again and shoot for the Top Ten.

"Thank you for catching the bad guy and protecting my honor against that dastardly devil," she smiled with that look in her eyes that always melted him.

"Actually, I saved him from a fate far worse than he's going to get at the hands of the judge," he said, almost ruefully.

Dana reached up and wrapped her lips around his left earlobe. "That's because you're the good guy," she whispered.

"Yeah, I guess. The police would have caught up to all of that eventually, though. These were petty criminals, not exactly evil at the level that demands a response from Mychus the Warrior."

"Oh, cripes, I gave up a long time ago trying to get through your skull," said a familiar voice from the general vicinity of the knickknack shelf. The Soulkeeper of Kiribati was checking in again.

"What?" Paul said, accustomed to having his romantic moments interrupted by a wise-cracking piece of pottery. "You think Astor City needed Myke Phoenix to break that up?"

"Wendell Hanrahan sure needed Myke tonight."

"Who is Wendell Hanrahan?"

"The serial kisser, you idiot," the vase said. "You didn't hang around to find out his name? He was about to be killed by an angry mob of men, some who never did anything stupid in their lives before and never will again."

"Oh, come on, they weren't going to kill him."

"Never underestimate the power of a mob to commit stupidity once they're riled up, especially when they've been riled up by the Forces of Evil in the World."

"What are you talking about?"

"Think about it, if you have any synapses at all snapping tonight," the vase said. "Three dozen guys are prepared to commit aggravated battery against a serial kisser? Why do you think they got so agitated? It's the Evil."

"That's kind of a weird way to show itself."

"You wait. It's just warming up."

The house was well-built and energy tight, but a chilly breeze crossed the living room and through Paul Phillips' bones.

"Come on, Paul," Dana said, tugging gently on his arms and leading him to the next room with a wary eye on the ugly green vase. "I'm feeling the urge for some serial kissing of my own."

About the author

I live in Door County not far from the shores of Green Bay, Wisconsin, with my wife Red, our golden retrievers Dejah Thoris Princess of Mars and Summer, and Blackberry the cat.

I (1953-) was raised in New Jersey but fell in love at first sight with the blue skies of Wisconsin, where I have spent my entire adulthood, first in radio news, then as a reporter/editor of community newspapers, more recently incorporating creative writing and book publishing into that mix.

In addition to being the mild-mannered editor of a local community paper and former owner-operator of a local independent online news site, I am the author of Full, 24 flashes, Gladness is Infectious, How to Play a Blue Guitar, A Bridge at Crossroads, Refuse to be Afraid, the Myke Phoenix series of novelettes, A Scream of Consciousness, and the science-fiction novellas The Imaginary Bomb and The Imaginary Revolution.

Please visit warrenbluhm.com for more!

Warren Bluhm

www.ingramcontent.com/pod-product-compliance
Lightning Source LLC
Chambersburg PA
CBHW030825200726